Time for a Rhyme

Contents first published by HarperCollins Children's Books in *Humpty Dumpty
and Other Nursery Favourites, Jack and Jill and Other Nursery Favourites* and
Twinkle, Twinkle, Little Star and Other Nursery Favourites in 2009, and
This Little Piggy and Other Action Rhymes and *Three Little Kittens
and Other Number Rhymes* in 2010
This edition produced exclusively for Bookstart

1 3 5 7 9 10 8 6 4 2

ISBN: 978-0-00-789197-9

HarperCollins Children's Books is a division of HarperCollins Publishers Ltd.

Visit our website at: www.harpercollins.co.uk

Printed and bound in China

HarperCollins Children's Books proudly supports Bookstart

Time for a Rhyme

Illustrated by Mandy Stanley

HarperCollins *Children's Books*

The Wheels on the Bus

The wheels on the bus

Go round and round,

Round and round,

Round and round.

The wheels on the bus

Go round and round,

All day long.

One, Two, Three, Four, Five

One, two, three, four, five,

Once I caught a fish alive;

Six, seven, eight, nine, ten,

Then I let it go again.

Why did you let it go?

Because it bit my finger so.

Which finger did it bite?

This little finger on the right.

Five Currant Buns

Five currant buns in a baker's shop,

Big and round with a cherry on the top.

Along came a boy with a penny one day,

Bought a currant bun and took it away.

Ring-a-Ring o'Roses

Ring-a-ring o'roses,

A pocket full of posies,

A-tishoo! A-tishoo!

We all fall down.

The Grand Old Duke of York

Oh, the grand old Duke of York,

He had ten thousand men;

He marched them up to the top of the hill,

And he marched them down again.

And when they were up, they were up,

And when they were down, they were down,

And when they were only halfway up,

They were neither up nor down.

Jack and Jill

Jack and Jill went up the hill

To fetch a pail of water.

Jack fell down and broke his crown,

And Jill came tumbling after!

Little Bo-Peep

Little Bo-Peep has lost her sheep,

And doesn't know where to find them;

Leave them alone, and they'll come home,

Bringing their tails behind them.

I Had a Little Nut Tree

I had a little nut tree,

Nothing would it bear

But a silver nutmeg

And a golden pear;

The King of Spain's daughter

Came to visit me,

And all for the sake

Of my little nut tree.

The Man in the Moon

The Man in the Moon

Looked out of the moon,

Looked out of the moon and said,

"'Tis time for all children on the earth

To think about getting to bed!"

Wee Willie Winkie

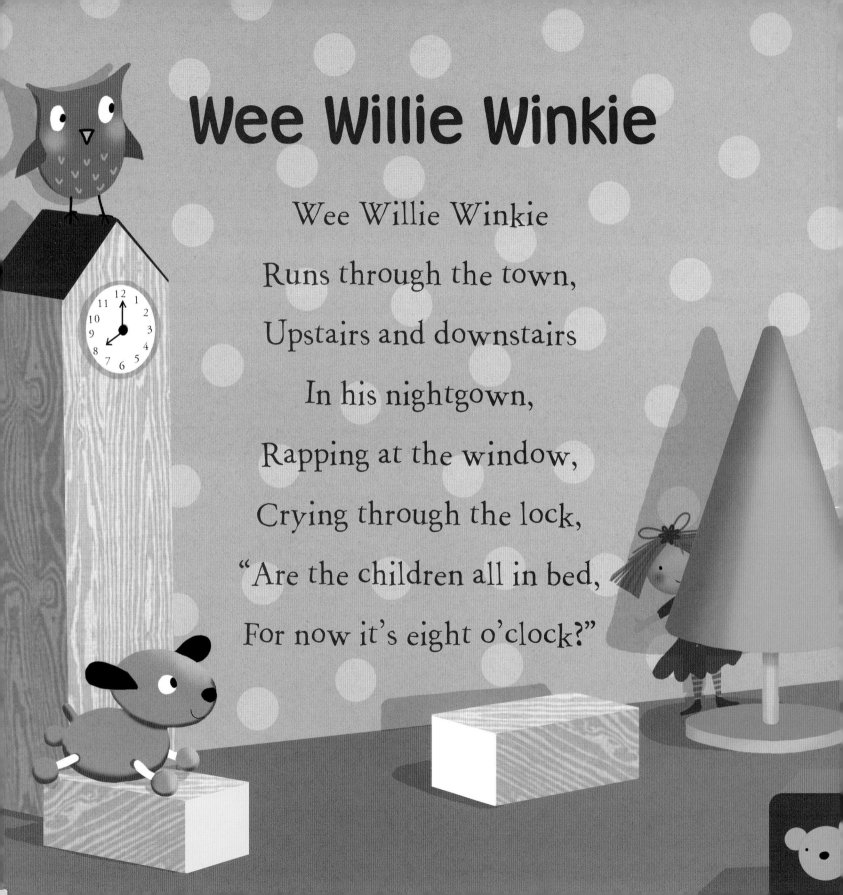

Wee Willie Winkie

Runs through the town,

Upstairs and downstairs

In his nightgown,

Rapping at the window,

Crying through the lock,

"Are the children all in bed,

For now it's eight o'clock?"

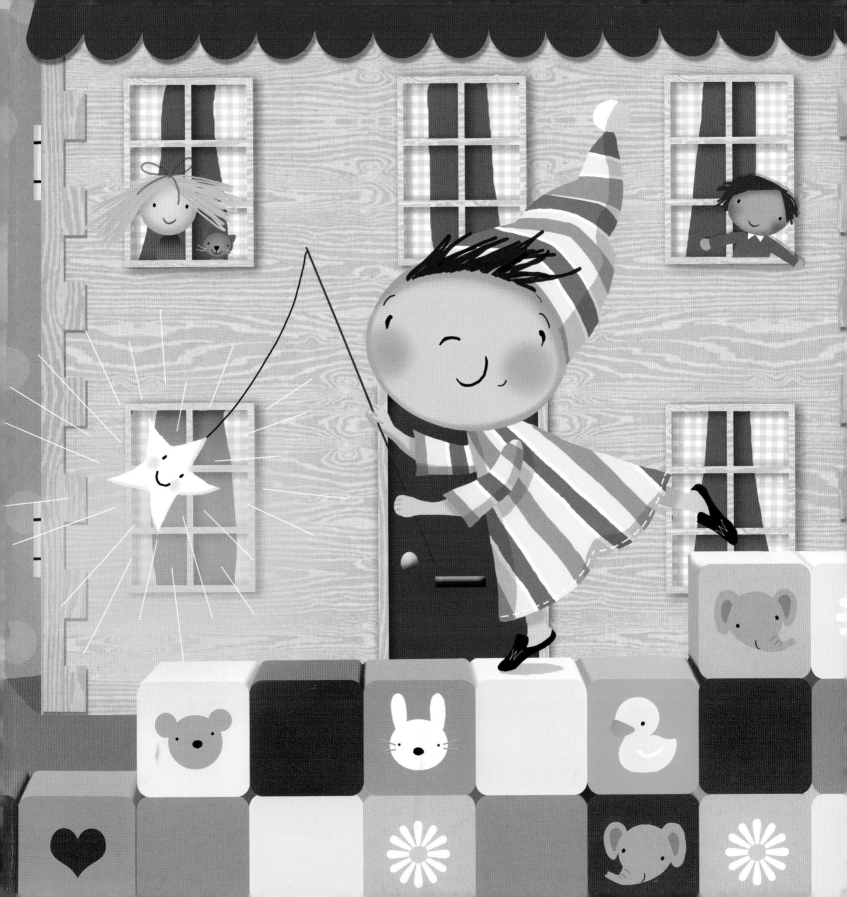

Now the Day is Over

Now the day is over,

Night is drawing nigh,

Shadows of the evening

Steal across the sky.

Now the darkness gathers,

Stars begin to peep,

Birds and beasts and flowers

Soon will be asleep.

Sabine Baring-Gould